LITTLE BLACK SAMBO

POOR LITTLE BLACK SAMBO WENT AWAY CRYING.

LITTLE
BLACK SAMBO

BY
HELEN BANNERMAN

PICTURES
BY
EULALIE

EDITED BY
WATTY PIPER

PLATT & MUNK PUBLISHERS/NEW YORK

QUESTOR ®
A QUESTOR COMPANY

THE STORY OF LITTLE BLACK SAMBO

Once upon a time there was a little boy from
India, and his name was Little Black Sambo.
And his mother was called Mama Sari.
And his father was called Papa Simbu.

And Mama Sari made him a beautiful
little red coat, and a pair of beautiful little
blue trousers.

And Papa Simbu went to the Bazaar, and

bought him a
beautiful green
umbrella, and a
lovely little pair
of purple shoes
with crimson
soles and crim-
son linings.

And then
wasn't Little
Black Sambo
grand?

So he put on
all his fine
clothes, and
went out for a
walk in the jun-
gle. And by and
by he met a tiger. And the tiger said to him,
"Little Black Sambo, I'm going to eat you up!"

And Little Black Sambo said, "Oh! Please
Mr. Tiger, don't eat me up, and I'll give you my
beautiful little red coat."

So the tiger said, "Very well, I won't eat

you this time, but you must give me your beautiful little red coat." So the tiger got poor Little Black Sambo's beautiful little red coat, and went away saying, "Now I'm the grandest tiger in the jungle."

And Little Black Sambo went on, and by and by he met another tiger, and it said to him, "Little Black Sambo, I'm going to eat you up!"

And Little Black Sambo said, "Oh! Please Mr.
Tiger, don't eat me up, and I'll give you my
beautiful little blue trousers."

So the tiger said, "Very well, I won't eat
you this time, but you must give me your beautiful little blue trousers." So the tiger got
poor Little Black Sambo's beautiful little blue

"OH! PLEASE MR. TIGER, DON'T EAT ME UP."

trousers, and went away saying, "Now I'm the grandest tiger in the jungle."

And Little Black Sambo went on and by and by he met another tiger, and it said to him, "Little Black Sambo, I'm going to eat you up!"

And Little Black Sambo said, "Oh! Please Mr. Tiger, don't eat me up, and I'll give you my beautiful little purple shoes with crimson soles and crimson linings."

But the tiger said, "What use would your shoes be to me? I've got four feet, and you've got only two; you haven't got enough shoes for me."

But Little Black Sambo said, "You could wear them on your ears."

"So I could," said the tiger. "That's a very good idea. Give them to me, and I won't eat you this time."

So the tiger got poor Little Black Sambo's beautiful little purple shoes with **crimson soles**

and crimson linings, and went away saying,
"Now I'm the grandest tiger in the jungle."

And by and by Little Black Sambo met another tiger and it said to him, "Little Black
Sambo, I'm going to eat you up!"

And Little Black Sambo said, "Oh! Please
Mr. Tiger, don't eat me up, and I'll give you my
beautiful green umbrella."

But the tiger said, "How can I carry an
umbrella, when I need all my paws for walking with?"

"You could tie it on your tail and carry
it that way," said Little Black Sambo.

"So I could," said the tiger. "Give it to me
and I won't eat you this time." So he got poor
Little Black Sambo's beautiful green umbrella,
and went away saying, "Now I'm the grandest
tiger in the jungle."

And poor Little Black Sambo went away
crying, because the cruel tigers had taken all
his fine clothes.

Presently he heard a horrible noise that
sounded like "G-r-r-r-r-rrrrrrr," and it got
louder and louder. "Oh, dear!" said Little
Black Sambo. "There are all the tigers coming
back to eat me up! What shall I do?" So he
ran quickly to a palm tree, and peeped round
it to see what the matter was.

And there he saw all the tigers fighting over
which of them was the grandest. And at last
they all got so angry that they jumped up and
took off all the fine clothes, and began
to tear each other with their claws, and bite
each other with their big white teeth.

AND THERE HE SAW ALL THE TIGERS FIGHTING.

And they came rolling and tumbling right to the foot of the very tree where Little Black Sambo was hiding, but he jumped quickly in behind another tree. And the tigers all caught hold of each other's tails, as they wrangled and scrambled, and so they found themselves in a ring round the tree.

Then, when the tigers were very wee and very far away, Little Black Sambo jumped up, and called out, "Oh, tigers! Why have you taken off all your nice clothes? Don't you want them any more?"

But the tigers only answered, "G-r-r-rrrrrr!"

Then Little Black Sambo said, "If you want them, say so, or I'll take them away."

But the tigers would not let go of each other's tails, and so they could only say "G-r-r-rrrrrrr!"

So Little Black Sambo put on all his fine clothes again and walked off.

And the tigers were very, very angry, but still they would not let go of each other's tails. And they were so angry, that they ran round

the tree, trying to eat each other up, and they
ran faster and faster, till they were whirling
round so fast you couldn't see their legs at all.

And they still ran faster and faster, till they
all just melted away, and there was nothing

left but a great big pool of melted butter (or "ghi" as it is called in India) round the foot of the tree.

Now Papa Simbu was just coming home from work, with a great big brass pot in his arms, and when he saw what was left of all the tigers he said, "Oh! What lovely melted butter!

I'll take that home to Mama Sari for her to cook with."

So he put it all into the great big brass pot,
and took it home to Mama Sari to cook with.
When Mama Sari saw the melted butter,

wasn't she pleased! "Now," she said, "we'll all have pancakes for supper!"

So she got flour and eggs and milk and sugar and butter, and she made a huge bowl of the most lovely pancakes. And she fried them in the melted butter which the tigers had made, and they were just as yellow and brown as little tigers.

And then they all sat down to supper. And Mama Sari ate twenty-seven pancakes, and Papa Simbu ate fifty-five, but Little Black Sambo ate a hundred and sixty-nine, because he was so hungry!